LIBERTY

By Vaughn Phelps

V. I. P.
PUBLISHING

COPYRIGHT 2014
ISBN #978-0-9838938-7-5
Published in America by V. I. P.

ACKNOWLEDGEMENTS

Cover design by Mitzi Michelle Phelps and
Jennifer Lydia Phelps
Edited by Ginny Greene

FOREWORD

I don't believe in giving too much away and I hate synopses, I think it's like conducting an autopsy while the patient is still alive and struggling to get off the table.   An introduction is like seeing the bride without her make-up, her hair still in curlers and her wedding dress hanging in the closet.

8

LIBERTY
TABLE OF CONTENTS

LIBERTY

STORY ADAPTED FROM THE ORIGINAL SCREENPLAY OF THE SAME NAME
By Vaughn Phelps

CHAPTER-1
LOST IN THE TENNESSEE MOUNTAINS

Sunlight finally breaks through the thick overgrowth of hardwood trees and the full impact of the disheveled yard and weather-beaten shack right out of a Lil' Abner cartoon are displayed in all their glory.   On the porch, a young man whittles a crude flute from mountain mesquite.   He tries it, enlarges a hole and tries it again. Another young man reads a month old *Wall Street Journal*, his bare feet propped against the railing.   In a rocking chair, an old man with gray-beard and unruly hair, picks at a banjo with spatulate fingers.   All three are dressed in holey bib overalls and torn wife-beater shirts. In the yard below, a large pink pig roots for mushrooms under a persimmon tree.

A young woman—who could easily be Daisy Mae except that her shoulder length hair is rich coffee brown, not blonde—comes from inside and yells, "Supper's on." The family members mosey toward the open door.   The pig is the first one in.

Moments later, a shiny new, customized van with Pennsylvania license plates enters the yard and stops. The engine noise dies and the driver's door opens. David, a handsome young man holds a map against the steering wheel. With a confused look, he reads, turns the map upside down, scratches his head then turns it around again. Looking out at the shack, he starts to step out of the van, but before he can get his foot on the ground and call for directions, three coonhounds, dripping water, rush from the noisy creek. All are covered with red mud. One lands in David's lap and with a hot tongue, licks his face. The other two squeeze into the back of the van where they shake, spraying mud and gunk over thick carpet, color TV, walnut cabinets and sleeping accommodations.

The young woman comes to the doorway, smiles and turns back inside. "Paw, y'all better come look at this."

Conservatively dressed in suede jacket and gabardine slacks, David steps out of the van holding his mud-splattered arms out at his sides. He too is now dripping river water. The gray-haired man comes to the door, looks out and smiles.

The woman takes a closer, more appraising look at this flatland stranger. "Y'all better wash up, mister, then come'n inside and git you some vittles." She turns back and is gone before he can respond.

Paw yells, "Tick, you an' Holler an' Hoot git from there."

He shakes his head and with little remorse in his voice or manner, he says, "Sorry mister, they's too friendly for lots'a folks. I reckon y'all better do like Shel says. Come'n take supper with us."

Shaking off as much of the mud and water as he can, David climbs the steps. On the porch, he removes his suede jacket and fits it over the back of the rocking chair, hoping, somehow, the mud will remove itself.

Before he can respond in the negative, the young woman comes out, takes him by the arm and leads him around the side of the house to a huge washbasin and a brick sized bar of homemade brown soap. She pumps water as he washes, then holds a worn towel till he's ready. Looking him over with a critical eye, she reaffirms her previous opinion. The impatient pig comes out and watches anxiously, as if to hurry them along.

"Okay, Maisie we's comin'."

David tries to explain his being here, wherever here is. "I'm looking for Liberty."

"Aren't we all? One way or another?"

"No, I meant Liberty, Tennessee."

"Yo're standin' on Liberty Hill, Tennessee, mister."

The interior of the shack is much larger than one would imagine from the external view, but it's broken into several rooms that tell nothing of their function. The three men sit at a large round table, knives and forks held as weapons. The young woman sets a huge cast-iron pot onto the table and without regard to manners, the men help themselves. The emphasis placed on eating, no words are wasted.

David takes a seat, not knowing whether to introduce himself or join the others by helping himself to food. The choices are reduced for him as most of the food disappears before he can pick up a fork. By the time the girl/woman seats herself on a milk can opposite him, only gravy, cornbread and a few morsels of meat that might well have been anything when alive, have survived the onslaught.

With the meal over, the men relax, push their chairs back, pick their teeth with large hunting knives, burp, then retire to the "parlor"—the general area around the pot bellied stove. The old man introduces his family to his guest. "This here is Luke. That other one is Clem an' my daughter here is Shel."

David takes the opportunity to finally identify himself. "I'm David. I got lost on these unmarked country roads."

The old man brings out a gallon jug. He takes the first swig and passes it around. Each take a swig. When it comes to David, he tries a tentative sip and his face reddens. With a voice hoarse from the almost pure corn liquor, he says, "I much appreciate your hospitality, but if you could just kindly direct me to the highway."

Shel comes over, wiping her hands on a flour sack apron. "Oh, you wouldn't git a handfulla yards from here in the dark without you'd git lost agin. In the mornin' we kin show you the way out'n these mountains. Don't you fret none. We kin easy put you up fer the night."

The jug comes around again, but David passes. Paw takes a swig out of turn then says.

"Course, the light o' my life may jest slip in with ya in the middle o' the night, but don't you pay her no never mind. If'en she pesters ya too much, jest you bite her on the ear. She hates that. Luke, you fix 'im up in the guest suite. Ah'm plumb tuckered out. In the mornin' Shel kin give ye directions. She's better at that writin' an' readin' stuff than the rest of us."

He wanders off to one of the back rooms, leaving the two boys and David by the fire. The woman is washing the rough clay dishes and the single pot, but she steals a glance in his direction every chance she gets.

Luke finally stretches, "I'm gonna turn in myownself. Com'n let's git you settled in."

David follows and views the bare cubicle he's being offered. With a conciliatory attitude, he voices, "You know, I have perfectly good sleeping accommodations in my van. I could easily make do."

"We mountain folk don't take kindly to havin' an offer to share our home rejected. We take it as a personal insult."

"Oh, I merely wished not to inconvenience you any further."

"Ain't nothin', we's always happy to share our blessings with a lost sojourner."

David looks around the bare room with built-in pallet bed and the chamber pot underneath, a shelf holding matches, a candleholder, and tin cup.

He tries to sleep, but at every little sound, he wakes with a start, expecting to see a young dark haired woman slipping under the hand-made quilt beside him.

CHAPTER-2
GUEST APPRECIATION

At dawn, the old man knocks on the wall beside the blanket-covered opening to David's cubicle. A sleepy-eyed David snuggles against a pink pig. The pig snores contentedly.

Before poking his head in, Paw says, "I warned ya that little sweetheart would find'ya. She always makes such a fuss over visitors."

David wakes, sees the pig and sits up with a start. It wakes the pig, which rolls half way over and gives him a big toothy grin.

"Come outten there, Maisie. Let the man have some privacy."

A procession of male heads looks in at David. In vertical ascension, they poke heads through the blanket opening. The three hounds on the bottom and the boys above. They offer a multiple "Mornin'."

The woman has washed David's clothes. They're clean, but wrinkled beyond belief. He gets fresh clothes from the van and changes. Outside, the old man is busy chopping firewood. Everyone but the old man and the girl are gone by the time David, dressed and shaved, enters the dining area. There is a heaping plate of bacon and eggs waiting when David takes a seat. The girl/woman pours two cups of coffee and joins him at the table.

She smiles coyly, "There's lots more a everything if'en yo're hungry." She points to the bacon. "If'en you want more of <u>that</u>, we calls it side meat.

Maisie's a bit sensitive, and even spellin' it gets her upset.   She always figgers it could be one of her relatives."

David looks up into Shel's large dark eyes, but sees no hint that he's being put on.   The judgmental look from the pig confirms the impression.

"My name's Michelle, but most folks call me Shelly or jest Shel."

"Why, Michelle is a beautiful name for a beautiful young woman.   I should feel quite honored to call you Michelle, if I may."

She blushes, "Don't hardly nobody call me that."

"It's settled then, Michelle it is."

"What kinda business brings you into these hills? You on your vacation?   You and…your wife?"

"No.   I'm interested in buying antiques, and I'm not married."

Not looking up, she says, "Oh, well you could'a left your fiancée someplace shoppin,' then gone off and gottcherself lost."

"No, no fiancée or girlfriend.   I'm afraid I got lost all by myself."

Smiling and sitting up straighter, she looks up.   "I could take you lotsa places right around here got antiques you could buy."

"Really?   That would be a big help.   I see no wedding ring on your finger.   How has one as lovely as you escaped matrimony?"

"Ah is a widow."

"Oh, I'm terribly sorry."

"Yeah, well, life goes on.   I'll jest finish up here an' we kin go."

The noonday sun is high and hot before David and Michelle have all the van's vertical surfaces sponged, the dried, cracked mud brushed from the carpeting and the blankets and sheets shaken and replaced. They have a quick lunch and prepare for a buying tour of the area.

CHAPTER-3
HOLLER TO HOLLER

Every culvert or gully, it seems, produces another shack—many within shouting distance, yet out of sight. At each place, Michelle shows him old farm implements, jugs, bottles, broken rockers, etc. She obviously has no concept of the distinction between valuable antiques and simply old things. David buys several small items, but nothing of any real value.

By the time they return to the shack it's dusk and darkness is rapidly falling upon them. In the yard, Clem throws a Frisbee for the pig, who catches it in mid air.

With a voice filled with ambiguity, David says, "I certainly thank you for your help. If you could just direct me."

"Sure. After the men folk have et."

She's gone from sight before he can respond. Even in broad daylight, following her directions, he'd been hopelessly lost. One dirt path is exactly like every other. Finding his way out in daylight might be difficult, but impossible in the dark. Glumly, he treads the steps to the porch.

Supper is prepared quickly and the rest of the family, with the attention that a physicist gives to detailing the formula for a hydrogen bomb, set about the chore of another wordlessly devoured meal. They adjourn once again to the pot bellied stove.

Passing the jug, Paw asks, "How did yo're day go, Davey?"

"All right. Michelle showed me around, but I was more interested in things of historic value."

"You mean like stuff from the War of Northern Aggression? Wasn't much fightin' round here. We're jest simple hill folk. All our men what wore the grey fought in battles off aways."

Michelle is quick to interject, "The onney heroes we got here is local ones. Davey Crockett, Dan'l Boone, Andrew Jackson like that. Don't reckon you'd be much interested in nonesuch?" She brings him a clean coffee mug and accidentally rubs a hip suggestively against him.

"Yes, oh yes. That's exactly the kind of thing I'm after. There's no reason not to tell you, I'm a professor of U.S. History and I'm always looking for esoteric items of interest for our department and the University Library. I've heard that some nice pieces have turned up from time to time in this part of the country."

Paw scratches his head and says, "Shucks, ole Shel here probly drug you all around showin' you beat-up old butter churns and wore out milk stools. She could'a jest as easy took ya to find that other stuff. If there's any of it aroun', Shel'll know who's got it. She's thick with all the Morgans and non-Morgans in these hills."

With pouty lips, Michelle comes to justify herself. "I could'a showed him that stuff taday, paw. I didn't know he wanted that kinda junk. He never said. Well, time enough tommory."

"Oh, I couldn't impose another night."

With a dismissive hand gesture, she smiles, "But it's dark again. You can't go now. In the mornin, I'll show you lots'a places where they got good junk. You know, the kinda stuff you're lookin' for." Yawning, "Well, night."

She and her father leave for their bedrooms. David watches her go. Out of hearing of the others, Michelle, takes her father aside. "He sure is purty, ain't he paw. Kin I keep 'im?"

"Now, Shel, you know when your MAW gits back she ain't gonna letcha have 'im for good an' all."

"I been thinkin' on that." And with her bright eyes gleaming, "I got it 'most worked out."

Seated by the stove, Luke and Clem sip from the jug. They alternate looks at David.

"Hope you ain't gittin soft on ole Shel."

"Yeah. Ain't none o' our business, but her bein' over the hill like she is, don't reckon she'll find nobody at her age. Nobody wants a gal over fifteen, an' she's more'n twenty."

"Yeah, it's too bad too. After what happened with her boy friend."

"Boy friend? You mean before or after she was widowed?"

They pass the jug to him.

"Widowed? Is that what she toldja?" Clem looks over at his brother, they both smile and head for bed, leaving the jug with David. In the cubicle he fights sleep late into the night, wondering how tactfully to get away in the morning.

24

CHAPTER-4
A MOUNTAIN TRAIL AT MIDNIGHT

With only moonlight to guide her, Michelle follows a narrow path through scrub oak and tall grass to a large tool shed.   It's well hidden from prying eyes by a tall hedge, planted like a moat, as if to protect the seemingly worthless building.

Early morning finds Michelle at the hot stove.   The men enter, yawning and stretching.   Michelle, in an effervescent mood says,   "Ah've got flapjacks this mornin', paw, jus like you like em, with blackberry jam. Sit yerself down."   Casually, without looking up she asks, "Where's yer guest?"

The old man gives her a suspicious look, but says nothing.   Clem and Luke finish eating and leave without a word.

Moments later, David enters, dressed in another ensemble of expensive blazer and slacks.

Michelle smiles coyly at him.   "Ah kept <u>ever'thing</u> warm for ya."

"I shouldn't."   Seeing the hurt look on Michelle's face, "Well, maybe just one hot cake."

The old man takes his hat and leaves.   He throws back over his shoulder,   "I figger on bein' home late."

After the first few bites, David says,   "I appreciate your offer, but I really should be getting on.   The items we found yesterday are really quite sufficient.   I had hoped, well, no matter."

With her back to him, "Ever what you say." She shrugs. "I'll show you on the map, soon's your ready to go."

After packing in three more pancakes and four cups of coffee, David asks, "I'd like to send you and your family a little thank you gift. What is your mailing address?"

"I'll write it down for you. It's kind'a involved."

Loading his things into the van's well-organized compartments, David, ready to leave, fidgets. "If you'll draw out those instructions for me, I'll get going." She leans into the van window.

"Let's see yer map." With a red marking pen, she starts a wavy line that makes about sixteen turns within the first inch. "Turn right at UNCLE ZEB'S corn patch, left at the burned out 'simmon tree, right at the muskrat ponds, right at the oak where Tick treed the six coons last month."

Along the margins she adds helpful notes. If ever he'd hoped to use the map for anything, it is now completely illegible.

"Give this jar o' apple butter to Aunt Loweeze when you go past her place. Actual, it looks complicated but once you get past there, you're just a spit an' a scratch from the highway. It's just getting' to her place that might be a problem. If only there was a way..." PAUSE. "Hey, I got it. I'll ride along withya to her place, then you can find your own way, no trouble. I'll sit an' jaw with her a spell, then come back with Cousin Ralph."

With a smile that brings out dimples he hadn't seen before, she jumps in beside him.

They travel quite a ways before she directs him to a cabin on the left. "This is one of the places I was goin' to show you. Since it's right on the way, we might as well stop."

It turns out to be a most fortuitous occasion. He buys a portable writing desk at least a hundred and fifty years old, some silver match safes from the colonial period, a snuff box even older, and some well made hand-fashioned knives at least ninety years old. She directs him to another stop. He finds silver buckles from the pre-colonial period, inkwells and quills still wrapped in newspaper from 1848. The next stop is Aunt Loweeze's place. There, he finds such a trove of treasures, he can hardy believe his good luck. The last items are two extremely old books.

Under his breath, to Michelle, "This reading primer is signed by Dan'l Boone and presented to his son."

Michelle, in a pouty mood says, "Oh well, you kin erase that stuff if'en you don't want it."

He gasps, "Oh no. I just paid her a hundred dollars for it. This next item is a bible with a genealogy table of the Morgan family and…"

Michelle takes that from him before he has a chance to ask the price.

"That's family goods. It's not for sale. You understan'?"

"Of course. I would like to look through it, though. There's a letter from General Washington, sending Col. Daniel Morgan to Quebec with Benedict Arnold and…"

"Oh, you kin have the letter. It's jes' to, not from any kin."

"Oh, I couldn't just…"

"There's one more place real close. If you wanna take a look 'fore you go. Ya are still goin?"

"Uh, yes, I suppose so. Perhaps you might go with me as far as the nearest post office. I could ship these things off. Then time would no longer be a factor."

CHAPTER-5
WARP & WOOF

The last stop is the best of all.   He spends most of his remaining cash on a book with part of a note from Robert E. Lee hidden behind the deteriorating paper lining.

> *Gen John Hunt Morgan,   Take your Morgan Raiders into Pennsylvania and there capture General Johnson.   Lee*

At the rural Kingsport Post Office, David ships the items off and makes a collect phone call to an associate. "Michael, I'm shipping some prize pieces, but I'm almost broke.   You're going to have to wire me some cash. Send it to the Knoxville Manor.   It's still light out.   I'll be checked in there by tonight."

They pass part of a Bed and Breakfast, The Southern Comfort, an elegant restaurant, and in an instant, he has a gem of an idea.   "Michelle, I'll send that thank you gift to your family when I return to Philadelphia. However, you've been so incredibly helpful, I hope you will allow me to buy you dinner here in this restaurant. It's rather a celebration, after all."

"Oh, David, you always look so nice, but ah'm not dressed fer no fancy place like that."

As serendipity, he has another idea.   "Up the street there's a women's wear shop.

We could buy you a dress and… Oh, but wouldn't your family worry if you weren't there to fix their meal?"

"I put critter stew on the fire. All they got to do is serve it up. They kin do that much theyownselves. Oh, David, could I really get a store bought dress?"

Smiling broadly, he answers. "I think that's the very least I could do for all your help."

Minutes later, inside the Cotton Picker Boutique, Michelle picks out an extremely short, low cut, bright red dress and holds it up for his approval.

"How's this?"

"Uh, are you sure you wouldn't like something a little more conservative?"

Crestfallen, "Okay, I jes' always wanted a red dress. It's my favorite color."

"Then by all means, you shall have it."

"But don'tcha have to have the right stuff underneath with something this fine?"

"Yes, well…"

He goes to obtain help. A well-dressed young black woman at the counter is wrapping a customer's package. She looks up and sees Michelle heading for the dressing room. The woman smiles, is about to say something, but is waved off by Michelle. They enter the dressing room together. In mere seconds, the woman emerges, goes to the lingerie section then returns to the dressing room with several articles and, behind the batwing doors, they are again gone from sight.

* * * * * *

At the University of Philadelphia History Department, Estelle, blonde, hard eyes and thin lips, stands before the desk, stamping her foot and pounding her fist on the counter. "Well if you won't tell me where he's gone, I'll just have to go see daddy." The receptionist rolls her eyes. Another clerk avoids confrontation by cowering behind a door.

* * * * * *

An entirely camera-ready Michelle emerges from the dressing room. Her hair is swept into a mass of thick waves of dark chocolate-colored hair with sparkling combs. She wears perfectly applied lipstick, eye make up and perfume. David is speechless at the transformation. She stands for his viewing pleasure as a beauty contest winner. The dress is form fitting and it's enveloping quite a form. There is only one flaw; the muddy boots. He sends the woman clerk for a selection of shoes and nylons. While they wait, David can hardly express his feelings. "Why, it's a miracle. I feel as though I've watched my baby sister grow up before my very eyes."

As she heads back into the dressing room with the shoes, under her breath, she mumbles,

Your baby sister, I ain't.

A moment later, she comes from the dressing room with black stockings and very shiny, very red, very high heels. She pulls up the short skirt even higher and looks down at her feet.

"Do you think these are too much?"

He pays the—not small town prices.   "Nothing else would do.   It seems I shall be escorting the most beautiful woman in town, perhaps the entire state, to dinner."

The black woman takes Michelle aside.   "Should I wrap up your other clothes, Shelly?"

"No, throw them out.   I'm through with them."

They start for the restaurant and Michelle takes his arm and, holding tightly, their bodies touch often and in several places.   She seems to have trouble walking in high heels so he walks slower than his normal pace.

CHAPTER-6
SOUTHERN COMFORT

At a front window table, he orders prime rib for them both. "Would you like wine with your meal?"

"If you think we ought."

He orders a locally labeled red wine and over a very leisurely dinner, they talk, laugh, and enjoy every phase of the evening together. Michelle, surprisingly, even seems to lose some of her mountain accent. When finally the meal is finished, she stands and David places most of his remaining cash on the table to cover the bill.

Picking up the nearly full bottle, she questions, "Did we pay for this whole big bottle of wine drink that we only used lessen half of?"

"Yes, but..."

Tucking it securely under her arm, she smiles and innocently slips her other arm into his. By accident her breast happens to rub against his arm more than once.

Heading for the van it's now as dark as ever dark has been, yet she seems in no hurry and he is unable to move her along. She must look into every shop window they pass. In over an hour they've toured only two-blocks of the two block town.

"I suppose we should be getting back, although I must admit I can't remember when I've enjoyed myself as much."

She gazes at him in horror. "Oh, we can't go home now. Strange cars aren't welcome in these mountains after sundown.

There's some independent business folks that work at night.   We just can't go home in the dark is all."

"But you'll be with me and…"

"That makes no never mind.   A dark night like this is called a Moonshiner's Night."

"But…what then?"

By happenstance, they have stopped again under the overhanging Southern Comfort Bed and Breakfast marquee.

"Don't they have some kind'a place where folks can stay over when they's away from home?"

"Wh…y, yes, this very hotel in fact, but…"

"Well, then that's what we'll have to do."

Luckily, the hotel accepts David's credit card. Booking two adjoining rooms on the second floor, he joins Michelle at the elevator and escorts her to her door. "I should call and let your father know the circumstances."

She giggles, "We don't have a telephone, silly."

"Oh.   Then I'll just get my shaving kit from the van.   I have a spare toothbrush and toothpaste."

She grabs his arm and pulls him to her.   "You'll be back?   You're not leavin' me here in this strange place?"

"No, of course not.   I'll be right back and check in to see that you're all right.   In any event I'll be right next door if you need me for anything."

At her door minutes later, David knocks and through the door's narrow opening, hands her the new toothpaste, toothbrush and hairbrush.

"Aren't you going to come in? We can have the rest of that wine stuff. Me bein' this far from home, I kinda' thought…"

"Yes, all right, just one glass, but then I'd better…"

On a nightstand, he sees two water glasses filled to the brim and shimmering with a deep red glow. When she shuts the door behind her, the sight of her captures his full attention. She stands—model posed, in black lace lingerie, stockings and red shoes.

"Michelle, you…you haven't any clothes on."

"I didn't want to wrinkle that nice new dress. 'Sides, I wear less than this in summertime and my brothers never say nothin' a'tall."

I however… He sighs. *…am not your brother.*

Sitting on the bed with one shapely leg crossed over the other, in one swallow she downs half her glass. David stands uncomfortably in the armchair and tries to avert his eyes. She pushes him back into the chair, leans over him, blocking his view of everything but cleavage.

"This under stuff ain't even cotton. It's so soft and smooth. Wanna feel?"

The draw is almost too much. All about him, her perfume lingers like a cloud from heaven. When she attempts to hand him his glass, it IS too much. He stands, mumbles an apology and starts for the door. She drains half her glass in a single swallow and; in one giant step, she is standing beside him.

Pulling open the adjoining door, she exclaims, "Look, there's this door. You can go right through to your room thisaway."

In the open doorway, a hesitant David turns to say good night.

She leans fully against him and presses her lips to his in an unsisterly kiss. "I must say, David, it has been a most pleasant evening. The most enjoyable I can remember in too long a time. Thank you."

With another, even warmer kiss, she heads back toward her bed. Half way there, she turns and in an offhanded motion, says, "Oh, you don't mind if I leave this door open do you? I mean, when I look out that window, I get dizzy, bein' so high up in the air. I'll feel more comfortable knowin' you is so close."

That same thought surely brings no comfort to David. Tossing and turning, sleep comes even harder for him than on the previous two nights.

CHAPTER-7
PHILADELPHIA?   NOT FOR SOME

Estelle pulls on her dress and looks down at Carlo, a naked, dark, sleazy looking man sitting up in bed.   She smiles,   "Now don't pout, darling.   It doesn't become you."

"But I don't see why we can't…"

"What we have together is marvelous, but it's purely physical.   After David and I are married and settled in, he'll get back to his boring history and I'll have my afternoons free.   I think a month should be long enough."

"You can't imagine that I would be part of such a thing?"

"Oh come on.   You weren't going to marry me anyway.   You only took interest in me at first, because I could find you some prize artifacts, well, I did.   I found you David.   With all your money, you can buy whatever you want of the junk he digs up."

* * * * * *

David and Michelle leave the hotel and join a dark, overcast morning.   Michelle is wearing the red dress and seems to walk much more comfortably in heels.   In fact, there is a sway to her hips he'd not noticed before.   She seems in no hurry and no matter how hard David tries to move her along.   She dawdles again in front of every store window.   Under her arm she carries two breakfast doggie bags.

FINALLY, they're in the van and heading away from this little pocket of civilization.

Sounding as if this is just another day, Michelle, with no enthusiasm says, "You might find something at cousin Alvin's place. It's just ahead."

They turn into a yard, and are greeted warmly by Cousin Alvin and shown a box of old books and papers. David opens a book of poetry with a note used as bookmark. He shuts it quickly and goes through the other papers, finding several other items of interest.

"I'd like to buy the contents of the whole box if that's possible."

Cousin Alvin is hesitant, but finally agrees to accept four times the expected price. David has to write a check.

Michelle leans over the rickety table. "That there check's good as Yankee gold."

Back in the van, David is all smiles. "I can't tell you how exciting this has been for me. Those papers…well I hesitate to speculate on their importance."

She pouts, "Huh, most mountain boys woulda tried takin' advantage of a girl in a situation like last night. And all you can talk about is…" She kicks at the box. "…this old junk."

Trying to keep his attention on his driving, and not looking across at her, he swallows. *Certainly not for lack of interest.*

CHAPTER-8
WELCOME HOME

Under the porch overhang, Clem, Luke and Paw sit in the partial shade. On guitar, banjo and wooden flute, they play a medley of Smoky Mountain melodies. The van pulls into the yard and Michelle is halfway out and on the ground when Paw reaches down nonchalantly, picks up an antique double-barreled shotgun and cocks both hammers.

TWO GUNSHOTS

ring out. Michelle jumps back into her seat. "Hurry, David, burn rubber."

He spins the wheel in a hard turn and is soon out of sight and gun range. "What is going on…?"

"Well, you DID keep me out all night. And look at the way you've got me dressed."

"But I can explain."

"Not to my Paw you can't. Not right now anyway."

"Well, what can we do? I have to…"

"I have kin all around here. Somebody will take me in."

She keeps him heading north. They try to stop at several places she directs him to, but each time, they are run off by gunshots.

"Word's made the rounds. But don't worry; they were the same way with my fiancée at first. They'll probably get over it in a while."

"I thought you said you were widowed."

"Oh.   I meant divorced."

They cross into Virginia just as a violent thunderstorm breaks and worsens as all daylight disappears, and the wipers can't keep up with the downpour.

"How could they have gotten the word about us? You say nobody has telephones in these parts."

"Mountain people have their own ways of communicatin.'   It's kind of like magic."

The van heads up a muddy road that is trying hard to be a river.   The rear wheels slide into a water-filled hole and the van is stuck good and fast.   There is no thought of staying and outlasting the storm in the warmth and comfort of the van as lightning bolts crisscross the sky. One flash of light shows the countryside and a barn, twenty yards away.

"There's a blanket under the seat.   If you'll wrap it around you, we'll make a run for it."

He takes an old yellow slicker from the closet as Michelle wraps up in the blanket and holds the food and her new shoes on her lap.

"You'll have to carry me.   I'm not going to get my new red dress muddy."

Not bothering to argue, he puts the slicker over her and lifts her out.   There is no point in running.   Before the car door is slammed shut he's as wet as he is going to be.

"Line me up with the barn at the next flash."

With her warm breath in his ear she whispers, "I never done this before, have you?"

They make their stumbling way to the barn in alternating snatches of bright light and complete darkness.

"No, I must say this is one experience I've missed until now."

"You make it sound like you're not enjoyin' yerself. You said just this morning how exciting things were."

"I had no idea, then, where the day would lead."

CHAPTER-9
FROM CABIN TO HOTEL TO BARN IN EASY STEPS

Finding a candle and matches, Michelle adds flickering light to the scene.

"Get those clothes off, David, and wrap up in this blanket before you catch your death."

"No, I'll be,"

SNEEZE

"…fine."

SNEEZE.

"Do as I say and don't be such a prude.   Else I'll have to undress you myself."

SNEEZE, SNEEZE…

"All…"

SNEEZE

"…right."

He goes behind a stack of hay bales.   When he comes out, wrapped in the blanket, Michelle has set their leftover breakfasts on an upturned bale, placed the candlestick in the middle.   Two other bales form seats. His clothes are hung over a beam to dry.

Hers are folded neatly on top of another bale.   She stands dressed just as the night before.

"I'm not going to get my new dress all wrinkled and full of hay."

"But, you can't…"

"Can't what, David?   Come and sit down.   We'll eat, talk and relax till the storm lets up."

They eat.   They talk.   He doesn't relax.   This seemingly normal situation lasts until the cold becomes too much, and they are forced to cuddle together in the blanket.   The storm lasts all night, but by morning, he seems to be much less hampered by convention.

Hearing male voices startles Michelle.   Through a crack between the wallboards, she sees men investigating the van and talking among themselves.

Whispering,   "Do you have a gun?"

"No, of course not.   I wouldn't shoot at your kin anyway."

She dresses hastily; motions him to do the same. "These are no kin of mine.   This is Virginia.   It's Carey country."

As the barn doors are thrown open, Michelle drives the two bearded men off with a pitchfork.   "Hurry, David; before they come back with their whole stinkin' clan."

She hands him the slicker, takes the blanket and heads for the van.   Whether by accident or intent, she knocks over the candle and behind them, a flame, small at first, licks it's way forward.   Due to the steep slope, the dusty ground is now bone dry.

They shove branches and rocks into the hole, and while the men are busy trying to suppress a potential conflagration, the van lifts out and they make a hard turn south.

"What are Carey's and why…"

"The Careys and the Morgans been feudin' for a hundred years or more.   Nobody remembers exactly why."

"You said your family would get over my keeping you out overnight.   Now I've got TWO nights to explain."

"Umm.   How would you explain it, David? Besides, I said it might take a while."

CHAPTER-10
TOURING THE MOUNTAINS BY VAN

As they pass through eastern Tennessee, Michelle, in her runway-ready outfit, directs him past the town of Boone. Looking over at him, she shakes her head and sighs, "David, it's a wonder you haven't been run off as a revenuer. Look at the way you're dressed. Well, I mean, not now, but when you look sharp like you usually do. Stop here at this farmhouse and buy some old clothes. I can show you a place near here with real historic items. It's an antique store and they know value, but if you find anything you like, they'll give us a good price. They're old friends."

At Morgantown, North Carolina, Michelle directs him to a small shop. As he changes into the worn bib overalls and a flannel shirt he'd paid designer prices for, she somehow manages to phone from inside the unattended antique shop. Not much later, an out-of-breath young girl opens the door of MORGAN'S MEMORIES for him and he enters the filled antique store. Before he gets halfway up the first aisle, he finds Andrew Jackson's private journal, describing the Battle of New Orleans. It includes a handwritten appraisal of $40,000.00, dated Nov 19, 1947 by Professor Van Ecklund from the University of Pennsylvania.

"This is something I'd very much like to purchase, but your price is a bit steep for me."

"Well," the girl says, "here in the boondocks we don't get many tourists passin' through with that kinda money.

They mostly wants post cards o' Elvis and pictures of Dolly Parton. That kinda stuff. How much ya willin' to pay for it mister?"

He bargains hard, and eventually agrees to a price of $15,000.00, subject to authentication. The woman accepts his check and agrees to hold it until he can arrange for University verification.

At a mom and pop store that accepts utility payments, offers driver's license renewals, ships and receives U.P.S. packages and offers holding facilities for vehicles, they allow David to use their landline to call the University. He asks for the immediate services of the head of the department to conduct the authentication.

Michelle paces and stews about something. "This van sticks out like a sore thumb. Nobody around here drives a thing like that."

"I have to get to Knoxville. I have money being sent to me there."

"I have kin hereabouts. We can borrow a car."

He pulls the van into the alley behind the antique store and stops at a row of private garages. Michelle jumps out and uses a key to open the first door. She backs a new Porsche Turbo 911 out and waves him to pull the van in. He closes and locks the doors on the van, bringing only a clothes bag.

To his questioning open mouth, she replies,"I use this car whenever I'm in town."

"Wow! Who's your kin, the governor?"

"Not this term." She drives through town heading west toward Knoxville.

David seems anxious. "I should stop and call, but it can wait until Knoxville. I can't really make any plans until I pick up that money."

CHAPTER-11
TRAVELING IN STYLE

The purr of the Porsche's Turbo engine is like having a big cat in the back seat as it pulls onto the lush but sedate grounds of the Knoxville Manor, obviously a hotel that caters to the elderly, idle rich. David, in his overalls and flannel shirt, moves to the registration desk. "You're holding a reservation for me. I'll need two rooms and…"

The clerk tries not to look too closely and never makes eye contact. "Impossible, sir."

"You mean you haven't two rooms for me?"

"I mean, <u>sir</u>, that we have no rooms for you."

"But I made reservations a month ago."

"Highly unlikely."

"Check your confirmed list."

"Oh, really now."

"No, you misunderstand. You <u>know</u> me. I've stayed here before."

With a dismissive smirk, "In better times, obviously."

"I can pay in advance, by either check or credit card. No, I'm over my limit on American Express, but…"

"Oh please, sir, don't beg." The clerk turns away from this unwanted person. Michelle appears and hears the last part of the exchange. To David, she says in a low voice. "I just checked the concierge desk. They have a message for you. I'll wait here."

"Yes, thank you. I won't be long."

As he rushes off, Michelle leans toward the clerk. "Checkin' in here, sport. One room, nothing too fancy."

She points a thumb at the retreating David. "He's with me." She signs the register M. Morgan with a fancy scroll. "Send a bucket of champagne to the room and mark it 'Compliments of the management.' Take it out of this." She reaches into her bra and pulls out a wad of crisp, new, hundred dollar bills. She hands him twelve. "We'll be dining in the big room and I don't want any hassle over signing the check. I'll pay any balance when we check out in the morning and you keep any overage. You got all that straight?"

He turns the registration form around and his eyebrows rise at the signature. "Yes, of course, and may I wish you and Mr. Morgan a pleasant stay?" He offers her two keys. She takes one. David returns, frowning. "There was no money, only a message. 'Surprise, from guess who'."

"What do you think it could be?"

He gives her a suspicious look.

"Hey, it's none of <u>my</u> people. A 20 gauge, to us, is subtle. We don't play those cutesy kind of games. Let's have dinner; I'm famished."

"But I have to change. It's a good thing I brought my own clothes."

"All right, but you look fine to me just the way you are." She hands him the key. "Guess I'm just stuck on you."

On their way to the elevator they pass behind a well-dressed blonde woman who keeps looking from the concierge desk to her watch. As the elevator closes, she goes again to the registration desk.

"I'm sorry, madam, as I've said before, there is no David Ross registered at this hotel. We had a reservation for him, but when he failed to arrive it was cancelled."

A short time later, when David and Michelle pass behind her into the main dining room, the blonde woman is still watching the front desk. While David moves to the house phone, Michelle orders dinner and a fine wine from a long list of expensive offerings. She orders in very fluent French. She is also an excellent dancer; but only accepts his invitation for the slow, touch dances.

Later, in the room, she frowns at the two beds and David makes another phone call to the same number. He is given only the message that a surprise awaits him in Knoxville. "I'm in Knoxville now, and the only surprise is that there's no cash waiting, as I requested. You couldn't possibly understand the awkward position that puts me in."

Michelle is hanging her dress in the closet as he slams the phone down. She removes the cork, pours champagne and hands him a glass. Again, she's dressed only in her skimpy lingerie and red heels. "Here, David. This will settle your nerves."

"It's a trade-off. You have a most unsettling effect on me."

She slips an arm around his neck and pulls his face down to hers. "You couldn't mean little ol' me, darlin.' I'm just a simple mountain girl, trying to keep up with a smooth talkin' city slicker." Her slow kiss implies that she's perhaps more than her words imply.

54

CHAPTER-12
AND A GOOD MORNIN' TO YOU

It's an animated Michelle who laughs and jokes with David over breakfast. The blonde woman, looking disheveled, paces and watches from the lobby. She'd had no reason, before, to pay attention when the bellman greeted Mr. and Mrs. Morgan. But then she sees David in the restaurant. He's smiling at something the woman has said to him. She pushes her way through the crowd and stands before their table. "David? I've been sitting in the lobby for two days."

Michelle, with a fast take on who this must be, says, "Really? This used to be a family hotel. I didn't know they allowed that sort of thing, but I guess the times, they are a changing."

With raised eyebrows, David says, "Estelle! What are you doing here?"

Turning to face Estelle, giving her a view of a trim but very curvaceous form, Michelle echoes, "Yes, Estelle, what ARE you doing here?"

"David, who is this person?"

"Go ahead, David, tell her."

Estelle can't turn her attention from the sight of a lot of nylon clad un-bumpkin-like leg.

"This is my guide. My mountain guide."

"You don't think I'm…"

"Oh, David, she's not going to believe that. Think of something else. Quick!"

"But it's the truth."

"Oh, David!"

"Oh, David."

Estelle stomps off. He gives Michelle a dirty look.

"What? Was it something I said?"

He rushes off after Estelle. "Estelle, wait, I can explain." He catches up to her at the concierge's desk where she is trying to make arrangements for transportation to the airport.

"Ah, good morning, Mr. Morgan. I trust you and your lovely wife had a pleasant evening?"

Michelle signs the dining room check and follows at a reasonable distance. The concierge is explaining to Estelle that the airport shuttle has just left. "I am sorry, Miss Petri. We can call for a taxi, but this time of day it will be half an hour or more. A shuttle to the train depot leaves in an hour."

"I just want the fastest way out of this horrid place."

"Ah, that would be the Greyhound bus depot. Or you may flag it down right across the street. That is, IF you know in which direction you are going."

Michelle strolls into the conversation. She smiles at David, "We could drop her off at the bus depot on our way. She might pick up some business. There are always plenty of service men from the nearby Army camp."

Michelle hands her car keys to the Concierge. "Would you bring our car around? It's the silver Turbo Carerra."

"Estelle, I had no idea you were coming down. I asked your father to wire me some cash and there was only a message that…"

"When daddy said you were down here in this God forsaken country and needed some cash, I thought I'd bring it down and surprise you."

Michelle tries with only limited success to keep from grinning. "Write us next time, Estelle. Let us know you're coming. That way we'll be better prepared for you."

David, with hope still in his heart, says, "Then, you've brought my money?"

Estelle gives him a poisonous look, "You must be joking." She storms off.

Michelle calls after her, "Wait, Estelle. We can make room for you in the back seat. You'll have to hold our luggage on your lap, but at least we can send you off properly."

David, with his arms in the air as if he's calling for Divine help says, "Michelle, what have you done?"

"You get our things and check us out. We'll go after her."

She dashes to the curb, where Estelle is trying to convince a cab driver just pulling up that he is the cab she ordered.

"Wait, Estelle. David didn't want to hurt your feelings and he certainly didn't want you to find out about us this way. At your age, you must have some leverage. You hold the mortgage on the family homestead or what?"

Estelle pokes the driver with a stiff finger and he pulls the cab away just as David rushes out from the lobby. "Where did…?"

"Oh, she left. She apologized for interfering, she could see that we only wanted to be alone."

"But we don't, I mean we're not…"

"I know, and I tried to explain that to her but she's so nervous and jittery. Is she always that way? Well, no matter. Did you get us checked out?"

"Yes, they said you paid last night. And thanks so much for the tip."

"Oh, that's right. I completely forgot. Paw has an account here. Well, I see you have our luggage, shall we go?"

He wears his own clothes, carries the overalls and shirt in one hand, two toothbrushes in the other.

She holds the Porsche keys out to him. "Would you like to drive, darling?"

His anger is quickly assuaged as he parallels U.S. 70 East.

It may not be The Smoky Mountains, but the silver Porsche is smokin' along at eighty-five miles per hour.

"It's just as well we didn't take her to the depot. Look at how depressed she's gotten you in just that little bit of time."

"She? She didn't…"

"Well, whatever. The point is, David, you're letting her bring the party down."

"This is not a party."

"It could be."

They top a crest of the road and look down onto a cluster of buildings. The arched sign over the gate proclaims modestly that this is the home of the WORLD'S FINEST TENNESSEE WALKERS. The brand is designated by a large silver-topped walking stick in the shape of a T resting in a rocking chair. David pulls to a stop before starting down the hill.

"Okay, tell me, before we get there.   Who's going to shoot at us this time?   Morgans or Careys?"

"Don't be silly, David.   Neither.   This is Tamerlane territory.   Besides it's Sunday, there's no fuedin' on Sundays.   We're God-fearing people in these mountains."

CHAPTER-13
WORLD'S FINEST TENNESSEE WALKERS

David seems unconvinced, but starts slowly down the slope. Within minutes, a shot rings out; he spins the car in a tight circle and retreats. He's getting better at it with practice; also the Turbo Carerra is far more responsive than his van.

"You said…"

"Oh, that's just Bud. He must still be sore. He wanted to marry me even before Ken."

"How did he know it was you? Those shots came from my side of the car."

David has not noticed the personalized North Carolina license plates, "SHEL."

"Just a lucky guess."

"Who's Ken?"

"He's the fella I was going to marry."

"Going to marry? You said you were widowed. Then you said you were divorced. The boys talked about a boy friend."

"It's a long story. Besides, I don't want to tell you with you all sore and testy about Estelle. I swear, a person would get the impression that I'd said something to make you angry."

"And a fascinating story it would be, I'm sure. That is, if you can ever remember to tell it the same way each time. But then maybe that's part of its charm. The way it changes and flows with the current."

They travel past more horse ranches.   None as large, well kept or impressive as the Rocking T, but then no one else shoots at them along the way.

After a long pause and several miles, in a calmer tone, he asks,   "Have you _ever_ been married?"

"No. Have you?"

"No."

"Engaged?"

"A couple of times. Estelle was the last."

"Well, you should be glad you're out of it. Everybody must have known that she was wrong for you."

He shakes his head. "It never seems to work out. I guess I'm not the marrying kind."

"Oh, you just never met the right woman before. Someone able to get you out of all kinds of trouble."

"I was never _in_ trouble before."

"Then I hope you appreciate how lucky you were to have found me just in time.   There may come a time when _I'm_ in trouble and need _your_ help."

They come to a small town and Michelle directs him to the Sheriff's office.

"Are you sure about this?"

"Trust me.   Haven't I been right about everything so far?"

Without giving him time to answer, she jumps out and enters the Sheriff's sub-station as David waits nervously in the car.

She returns, smiling broadly.   "We can go home now. I fixed it."

At his look of disbelief she waves her hand in a shooing motion. "Go, go, go."

"How did you…"

"Mountain ways.   You probably wouldn't understand."

He doesn't see the high-masted short-wave antennae tower above the sheriff's station.

CHAPTER-14
UNEXPECTED FAMILY GREETING

At the shack, Michelle's family comes out to greet them.   A shotgun is propped against the porch rail but nobody makes a move toward it.   Not until they're out of the car and shaking hands does David see the Sheriff and the minister on the porch.

An aside to Michelle,   "I thought you said you fixed it."

She slips her arm into his.   "I did.   This's how we fix such things in the mountains.   Would you prefer dodging buckshot for the rest of your life?   'Course, maybe you can explain to the sheriff about taking me across the state line for immoral purposes.   I think that's called the Manly Act.   Or checking us into a hotel as man and wife?"

"I didn't check us in, YOU did."

"I know, but they'd never make that distinction."

"I'll show them the receipt from the hotel."

"Details."

"I'll make them believe it."

"That's a good idea.   Who signed us out?"

"Oh."

The impromptu wedding goes off without a hitch. The bride and groom run for the car, find the three dogs and the pig sitting patiently in the back seat. Maisie grins. She wears a white bow around her neck.

"Maisie, you come out of there and bring those hounds with you.   You know you can't go on a honeymoon.   T'aint proper."

The pig leads the three dogs off in a column.   All hang their heads in dejected fashion.

Michelle holds her hand out for the car keys and says, "I'll drive, darling."

"To where?   Oh well, it doesn't matter.   My life is over."

"You're just feeling the Wedding Jitters.   Lots of grooms get it."

As the Porsche tools along, the dark cloud that portends a storm seems as if it's following them.   David pays no attention to road signs and doesn't recognize the place when they arrive back in Morgantown.   It's almost as dark as being in a closet, and after a series of twists and turns through town, Michelle parks in the back alley beside the garage where the van is parked.   She leads him to an iron grille-covered entrance.   Like a man lost in a time warp, he follows her up the stairs to an apartment above MORGAN'S MEMORIES, the antique store from their last visit.

CHAPTER-15
HONEYMOON GET-AWAY

Locking the door behind them, Michelle listens to an answering machine as she looks through a stack of mail. "I'll just put on an apron before fixing dinner. I don't want to get my wedding dress dirty."

Inside the bedroom, she takes off the red dress and puts on a skimpy black lace apron that covers very little of either her lingerie or herself. With the dress on a hanger she forces it into a closet filled with Paris labeled clothes. There are at least a dozen expensive red dresses.

After a meal of microwave-thawed frozen dinners and a bottle of fine French Bordeaux, she shows him around the European antique-filled apartment. They end in the modern bedroom.

David is impressed, but standoffish, "You know, of course, that wedding will never stand up in a court of law."

The apron drops to the floor as she slides her arms around his neck.

"We're not in court."

She snaps her fingers and the harsh overhead becomes a soft bedside light beside a round waterbed.

"But if you intend to reject a Morgan, in the heart of the Morgan Mountains, to a Sheriff named Morgan, I suggest you get a good night's sleep and tackle the problem in the morning when you're rested and fresh."

Their lips meet just as the stereo comes on with violin music and the light dims even more.

David, propped in bed, is covered with a red sheet. He lifts the sheet and discovers that he's still dressed; that is if wearing only cashmere sox can be considered dressed. He doesn't look rested. He dials a bedside wireless phone and listens to a full recitation of recent events. "I appreciate your help, Dr. Styvasant."

Michelle enters with a breakfast tray. She's wearing a more demure full apron, or at least it would be demure, if she wore anything under it. Setting the tray over him, she tucks a napkin under his chin. It slides off.

"Then you haven't gotten to the important pieces yet?"

She leaves, returns with a roll of shipping tape, pulls off six inches and tapes the napkin to his bare chest. Hot coffee spills onto his lap. He drops the phone. Michelle rolls on the floor in a mirthful fit. When it subsides, she feigns indignation and lifts the tray from the bed.

Into the retrieved phone, he continues. "I'm sorry professor. I just had an accident with a hot phone and dropped the coffee."

Michelle returns for the napkin, jerks it from his chest, pulling a swath of hair with it. David howls and she manages not to laugh, almost.

"Sorry again, professor. Would you mind repeating that last part?"

Michelle comes to sit beside him and turns the phone so that she can hear.

"We've done a preliminary and I find no problems with anything. But then the main trouble may come from another source.

I have no idea what happened, but Estelle was in here this morning trying to use her influence to force us into finding the items forgeries."

Rubbing his forehead and squinting, David tries to put a positive spin on the situation. "She found things down here not exactly to her liking."

"You must have had the devil of a row. She's threatened to have her father use sanctions against you and all those who have helped you, past or present. For those of us with tenure, that's just laughable. But I'm afraid that you, my boy, might be in trouble."

"You don't know the half of it. But thank you, professor. I'll handle things and, again I most appreciate your support."

"Not at all, my boy. You may have lucked onto the pieces that will make you financially independent of Estelle's pressure. That is, if it's what you want. Frankly, I always thought you could have done much better."

Forcefully, Michelle nods her head.

"For what it's worth, I get the strong impression that she would forgive you your little fling if you came back right now and apologized."

Michelle holds her nose and makes a castaway motion with her other hand.

"Well, good day to you."

As David hangs up, she dives away as he grabs for her. She's out of his reach, all but her ankle. He gets a hold, drags her back, holds her down and tickles her. When finally she's too weak from laughing to even struggle, it ends in an embrace.

An epiphany comes to him while she's wrapped in his arms and her face is resting comfortably against his chest.

As good as she smells now is because of some probably very expensive perfume, but even back at the shack, she smelled just as good.

The morning is cloudless, as they walk back along the main thoroughfare and stop at a French sidewalk cafe. They order coffee and croissants. Michelle argues in French with the waitress that his croissant is not fresh. She sends it back. The owner comes out. She argues with him, and finally receives satisfaction. On the back of a menu she doodles, "Antique Store for Sale, including four warehouses full of inventory, mostly French."

It's such a warm, bright, sunlit day that she takes him for a stroll around town. Wearing an expensive bone-colored knit dress that shows off her complexion and dark hair, she has no problem walking in the five-inch heels of her six hundred dollar alligator shoes. At one entrance is a statue of Daniel Boone. At the other, is one of Davey Crockett. Almost as if the scene had been choreographed by Hollywood, Songbirds serenade them wherever they go throughout the park. With ice cream cones, they end on a park bench, enjoying the weather's soft breeze, and each other.

In the middle of the park, they pass a much larger statue of Captain Henry Morgan.

Even though she keeps her arm linked with his, she keeps her head down and avoids looking directly at him. "There are things about me you probably want to know?"

"Are you sure you want to tell me? I kind of like you just the way you are, and every time you talk about yourself, your nose seems to grow an inch."

She digs an elbow into his side, but hides her smile from him.

CHAPTER-16
SECRETS REVEALED?

Back at the apartment, Michelle seems nervous. "I have to go out for a bit. Do you mind waiting for me here alone?"

"Without a car, where else am I going?"

She kisses him and leaves quickly. David phones the University. Busy. He washes dishes and tries to think of a winning plan. He's so absorbed in his thoughts that when the phone

RINGS.

He can't remember where he's left the cordless unit. Finally he picks up the combination telephone and message recorder. "Hello."

A man's filtered voice asks, "Who the hell are you? Where's Shelly?"

"I'm afraid she's not in at present. May I…"

CLICK.

Michelle's filtered voice comes over the receiver. "I have it, darling. You can hang up now, thanks."

"Where are you? I thought you'd already left."

"I'll be home soon."

David hangs up the phone, but it's a speakerphone and hanging up doesn't disconnect it. He hears the rest of the conversation.

"Who was that, Shel? Sounded like some wimp."

From downstairs in the Antique shop, Michelle answers. "He's my husband."

"You told me that once before. It wasn't true then, so why should I believe you this time?"

"Because this time it is true. Besides, you know I never loved you, Bud. We could be friends, nothing more."

"No, not friends, Shelly. And we'll see just how true it is this time. Is he Morgan or Carey?"

"He's neither. He has breeding and class."

"So do my horses."

"It's a shame none of it ever rubbed off on you."

In the apartment, David finds the off button. The phone and apartment go silent, but it only disconnects the apartment phone, not the extension phone in the shop below.

Michelle says, "He's not mixed up in this. Besides, this feuding is all nonsense. Nobody's been shot in over twenty years. It's just foolish macho pride. It wastes energy, and cuts into profits."

"You know as well as I do, it's all part of the image. Almost as important as the…"

She hangs up.

In a petite French restaurant, David and Michelle are dressed for dinner in Manhattan. Over chateaubriand and a vintage bottle of Petit Sherae, she takes on a slower, more direct expression and she launches a serious matter. "I know we have to talk, David, but I'm having such a marvelous time right now please don't spoil it for me. There's time in the morning."

Her smile is as wistful as a girl asking Santa for just a small doll.

The string ensemble plays softly, and holding her close through a single dance, he's in no mood to spoil anything.

Hand in hand, as they walk back to the apartment, David keeps stealing glances at her.   His mind is obviously working, but it's hard to tell whether he is trying to visualize this stunning creature as he first saw her or trying to imagine how she might look in tweeds and holding a delicate teacup at a faculty get-together.

CHAPTER-17
BREAKUP?

David makes breakfast, brings it to the bed and fluffs Michelle's pillow. She refuses to look up at him as she says, "Your van is ready whenever you want it, David. I had it washed and serviced. It's parked just half a block away."

"Oh, there's no great urgency."

"Last chance, David. There are things about me that you should probably ought to want to know."

"Well, as long as you're playing the role, every bride is entitled to her few little secrets."

When she hears him busy in the kitchen, she reaches three times for the cordless phone, but recants. The fourth time she dials a seven-digit number. "Did you get that information I asked for?" PAUSE. "Thanks, you're a dear."

At the Sub-Station, the Sheriff smiles and hangs up the phone.

Michelle copies a ten-digit number on a pad of paper, jumps up and takes her shower. While she's in the bathroom, David enters the bedroom, reaches for his reading glasses on the headboard seeing the note pad and phone number. He smiles and whistles as he's dressing.

Michelle, fitting earrings in place, passes him in the living room. "I have to go out for a teeny bit. Do you need anything?"

David shakes his head and she skips out the door.

Moments later, the red light on the speakerphone comes on. David waits a minute then pushes the on button. Michelle's soft voice fills the room. He turns the volume down.

"Mrs. Ross? I know this is a strange introduction but I'm Mrs. Ross also. David and I were married Sunday."

"You were what, married?"

"Yes, I know, I was surprised myself. But David can be so impulsive at times"

"My David ? Are you sure we're talking about the same person?"

"Yes, your David. Professor David Ross. Well anyway, he sprang it on me so suddenly we didn't have a chance to notify anyone. He felt so uncomfortable about your missing the wedding; I just couldn't remain reticent. We've decided to go through it all over again, more formally this time."

"You're serious?"

"Of course. Tomorrow afternoon at three o'clock. The Chapel For The Wayward Traveler. Knoxville is only an hour's flight. I'll wire you the tickets and my folks can pick you up at the airport. They're so looking forward to meeting you."

"Well, I've waited for this day for years. I'm sure I'll love you just as much as David. Wait, you're not that...not that...Estelle, are you?"

Michelle laughs. "No, ma'am, I'm Michelle Morgan, oops, Michelle Ross."

"Oh thank heavens."

"Thank you, Mrs...."

"Marianne, dear, but you can just call me Mom."

In the antique store below, she hangs up the phone and, smiling, throws out a two weeks accumulation of junk mail. She hums, "Here Comes The Bride."

In the apartment above, David hears Michelle hang up. He has a conversation of his own with his mother.

* * * * * *

At the same time, "Maw," an attractive, older version of Michelle, parks a new Mercedes-Benz S Class sedan in a stand-alone garage, covered as well as if a camouflage expert had designed it.

At the shack, her family greets her and helps her carry packages into the shack. All have Paris labels. "I swear, Paw, we should sell that place. I just can't get good help on the Riviera anymore. Especially when we only keep it open for a few months a year. I should have insisted on Shel going along as usual. I never did enjoy traveling alone."

Paw hands her a bone-china cup of steaming, fresh ground Sumatra coffee. "Thanks, darling. Did anything exciting new happen while I was gone?"

He smiles and changes the subject. "I've prepared some of your favorites for dinner. We will start with Pate Maison and Coeurs de Palmiers Vinaigrette. Then Carre d'Agneau Bouquetiere, pour deux. The boys have errands to take care of, so they won't be joining us. For dessert, Mousse au Chocolat. After we've eaten, I'll fill you in on current events in the hot tub over Napoleon brandy."

They pass the rough cubicles and through a secret door, enter a gourmet kitchen in gleaming stainless steel.

The Danish modern dining table holds lit candles in sterling candelabra and red roses in a cut glass vase.

CHAPTER-18
HAPPY LANDINGS?

The first class section deplaning first, Mrs. Marianne Ross steps onto the ground and looks around. She's not sure what to expect, but certainly not the couple dressed and looking like ambassador and queen standing beside a new Rolls Silver Cloud. Paw, clean-shaven and in a tailored tux—and girdle, is a dashing figure. He says, "Mrs. Ross? Why, if it weren't for the striking resemblance, we would never have recognized you. You have the same startling blue eyes as your son David. But we were expecting a woman old enough to have a grown son."

He kisses her hand and Mrs. Morgan motions for Clem, also cleaned up and wearing a tux and patent leather shoes, to get the bags and help their guest into the back seat.

Maw says, "We've taken a suite for you at the Knoxville Manor. I thought you might want to freshen up a bit. Then after the wedding, we can get to know each other over dinner. They have a fine French chef. I recommended him myself."

Clem drives them to the hotel.

Held back by the press of pushing and poking economy and business class travelers from the same flight, Estelle fights to reach the last taxi, but she's too late and waits impatiently for the shuttle to town. Bud watches from the gate. He sees the Morgans drive off and notices the woman trying desperately to find someone. He moves to intercept her.

"Pardon me, miss, I couldn't help but notice. It looks as if you may have missed the same people I did."

"You, you were also looking for Mrs. Ross?"

"Mrs. Ross? Yes. Seems we just missed her. You're here for…?"

"The wedding. Or so they think."

Hardly believing his luck, he says. "My car is just over there. Perhaps I could offer you a ride? Local taxis leave much to be desired."

"I know all too well your public transportation system, but…"

He points to a new Corvette.

"Well, I would appreciate a lift."

She slides into the deep glove-leather seat and they drive off with the deep-throated roar that only the tuned muffler of a racecar makes.

"We'll just stop off at my place and contact the Morgans. We can tell them you're here for the occasion."

"Why didn't we just phone from the airport?"

"They haven't a phone. We have to use the radio. It's the most efficient form of communication around these mountains."

"I see."

Bud drives through the wide and high bronze gates of Tamerlane Farms. Estelle shows more interest as she sees the large house, the pastures with prancing horses and the well-attended grounds. Bud escorts her through a side entrance into a comfortable, but obviously male oriented den. He turns on a large elaborate short-wave radio set. At a liquor cabinet, he fills two large glasses.

"Have to let the radio warm up.   Meanwhile, Martini & Rossi?"

She nods, "Mmm, my two favorite Italians."

Bud eventually tries the radio.   His call to the Morgans is unanswered."   They drink and try not to be too obvious in their observation of each other.   He turns on the stereo, puts on a Rigoletto album and returns to the couch. "I hope you enjoy Pavarotti?"

"Umm, my third favorite Italian."

His next radio try is successful.

* * * * * *

Luke, also looking very handsome in a tailored Italian suit, monitors the radio, and a recording answers with, "Hello caller, I'm the only one here and I'm on my way out the door.   Going to my sister's wedding."

* * * * * *

Bud tries to respond, "Tell that…" "Wait, where are your folks?   I'd like to offer my congratulations.   I'm an old family friend."

CLICK.

Getting only a repeat of the outgoing message when he tries again, Bud tries the county Sheriff.   He gets the deputy and asks the same question.

"Is that you, Bud?   Now you know Shel don't want you there.   We all know you'll start trouble.   I'm not at all sure I should tell you."

"Cousin Sonny, as I remember, you wanted to borrow my Corvette to take Betty Sue to her prom."

"It's the Knoxville Manor, where I'm going now. The pre-nuptial party is there. May I tell them you're coming?"

"No, I'll be in the audience at the happy event and I'll make my presence known at that time. Let's see, it's at…?"

"The Chapel for the Wayward Traveler, in Asheville."

"Thank you. Out."

Back on the couch beside Estelle, he refills their glasses and asks, "Are you a friend of the groom then? Here to see the couple happily joined?"

"Hardly that. I'm engaged to David. This woman must have cast a Devil's spell over him."

"Yes, she can do that. Would you excuse me for a moment?" He walks through the main hall, into the large living room and heads for the phone. Estelle moves to the door where she can watch him and sees the extension phone. She picks it up and hears the ring, then Michelle's voice. It's her answering machine telling the caller, in a soft and sedate calm tone, to "leave a message." At the tone, Bud leaves his message.

"Tell that wuss you're with, that I have his girl friend, and if he ever wants to see her again he'd better call off this nonsense."

Estelle eases the phone onto the cradle, stands looking out through the picture window at a lovely pastoral scene. A man on horseback leads another large golden-colored horse and ties it to the hitching rail by the side door.

He then rides around to the front of the house and out of her sight.   Entering the front door, he waves agitatedly to Bud.

"What's got you so riled up, little brother?"

"That Louisville outfit was supposed to ship my fancy new tack the fastest way.   They did. Greyhound. 'Cept now I've got to pick it up at the depot."

He tears open a package and with disgust, shows the apple green and orange satin shirt.

"Does this look like something I'd wear to Founder's Day Parade?   It's something a waitress at Hooters might look good in."

"Calm down.   We can fix it.   I'll call them right now."

"There's not time.   The show's this weekend.   I was gonna take it back in person, but my truck sounds like it's missing on four cylinders.   All the other cars are gone.   Can I borrow your Vette?   I'll be back in about an hour."

"Sure, sure."

"Thanks.   Oh, Truman's out front, and Temptress is at the side.   If you ride her, be sure you tighten the cinch. I just slipped the saddle on to try the fancy goo gaws. Bye."

CHAPTER-19
FUN WHILE IT LASTED

The crowd makes way for Mrs. Ross and the Morgans as they enter the hotel. Many say hello and several shake their hands. On first name basis with two state senators, one past governor, the new ambassador to Thailand and the junior U.S. Representative, Paw introduces Mrs. Ross. They enter a flower-filled, lavish buffet-set banquet room. Mrs. Ross smiles at Mrs. Morgan.

"That is such an attractive dress. I've been admiring it since we first met."

"Thank you. I bring back a few new things every trip, needed or not. I think it a crime to travel the continent without shopping for a few creature comforts. It keeps life from becoming a bore. Do you know Paris well?"

"I've never been. I've always wanted to travel, but, something else always came up."

"Then, you must come with me on the next trip. I don't enjoy traveling alone and now, with Shelly married…"

"Oh, I don't know. It was a problem in the past and now I'm afraid it may be out of the question."

"Why is that, Marianne?"

"It's David. He enjoys his work at the University and he was looking forward to tenure. But there are those, I'm afraid, who hold animosity toward him. Some did not take kindly to this marriage."

"The Morgans founded the University of Tennessee at Morgantown.

We still sit on the Board of Regents there. I'm sure if he wanted it, there would be an opening as head of the History Department. But if not, we have some influence with several major centers of learning here and abroad. We'll see what David has in mind after he's had a chance to discuss it with Shelly."

* * * * * *

At the French Restaurant, David and Michelle finish a late brunch and ease their way back to the apartment. She looks over her mail. David turns on the CD and reads the newspaper. When he enters the bathroom, she checks her phone messages and smiles. While the water runs, David dials the wireless phone.

Dr. Styvasant answers. "The books are all authentic, my boy. Binding, paper, ink, signature. All the known tests. That's the good news. Now for the bad news. At least from the University's standpoint. Carlo Falarri, you know, that fellow Estelle brought around a couple of times? The one who always wants us to sell him items from the archives? Well, he found out about the Jackson piece. He's gone over my head and made a written one hundred seventy-five thousand dollar offer directly to the board of Regents for the Jackson piece. The University could only go as high as the appraised value of forty thousand, even if that appraisal is out of date. I know we'd both like to see it on display here but you must sell it where you can get the highest price and this person wants to buy many more such items." He touches lovingly the book on his desk. The wrappings show that it's just recently been received from David.

"Thank you, professor; I should be back shortly. Your help has been invaluable."

"Not at all, my boy. Take care of yourself. We'll see you when you return." He hangs up and then smacks his head.

My heavens, STYVY, you're getting to be a regular absent-minded professor. You forgot to tell him that Estelle is on her way down there. Well, he'll know soon enough.

At the apartment, Michelle pulls a short white lace dress over her head as David comes into the bedroom. "David, we have a family get-together I forgot to tell you about earlier. Would you change into the things I've laid out for you, please?"

* * * * * *

Knowing she's to be held captive, Estelle tries to figure a way out. She sees the Corvette drive off, but Bud returns before she can devise a plan.

"Let me freshen your drink." He refills her glass.

"Oh, I sheally rouldn't. I get giddy with more than one glass, and I've had..." She giggles and holds up three fingers, then forces one down, ... "two already." She slides over on the couch toward him. Their thighs touch. "But shouldn't we be getting on to the shurch? Where is it, by the way?"

"The Chapel for the Wayward Traveler, but we've plenty of time."

She leans forward, presses her breasts against his chest and slips a hand under his coat.

"Well, in that case." She slurs, "Why don't you take your jacket off and make us boff more comfable? Iss a nice jacket."

As he leans forward to slip his arms out, she raises her lips to within an inch of his. He kisses her, then again. With his jacket off, he slides a powerful arm around her waist, pulls her to him.

"Now thass more like Souvern Hostapalty."

With her arm around his neck, he's encouraged, and tries to pull her under him.

"Not so rough. You're so masculine you don' know your own strenmth."

He slides a hand to her knee. After several more kisses, she pulls back and stands. Slipping off her bolero jacket, she steps out of her shoes.

"Is there somewhere to freshen up?"

She picks up her shoes, takes off her earrings and smiles coyly.

"Through that door, to the left. Don't be long."

She sways her way to the door. Bud goes to the picture window, reaches for the draw drapes, but sees her running out the side door and toward the tethered horse. In a minute, she's in Temptress's saddle, kicking the horse and pulling it in a turn away from the house. The horse moves at an easy gait.

"Move, giddap, run, gallop, go."

Lifting his legs high and arching his neck, the horse keeps to a predetermined slow pace, ignoring her impassioned pleas.

"Damn walking horses."

Astride Truman, Bud easily gains on her. As she tops the crest of a rolling hill, she comes abreast a stable. The horse makes an abrupt right turn.

90

The saddle and rider only make a partial turn. Estelle is dumped on her rear. Bud is off his horse in seconds. He feels her for broken bones. Not every place he feels has bones. He picks her up and easily carries her into the stable. Easing her onto a pile of fresh hay, he undoes her belt and unbuttons her blouse.

"What do you think you're doing?"

"First aid training says to loosen all restrictive clothing."

"That's for concussion, drowning or asphyxiation. I fell on my, well, I didn't fall on my head."

She tries to push him off but his arm is a large as her thigh.

"You're so physical. If only David were…"

She looks up into his eyes, sighs and pulls him down on top of her.

CHAPTER-20
COUNTING COUP

David fusses about his clothes time after time while Michelle grows more nervous as the minutes speed onward.

She checks her watch every few seconds. "David would you please come on. Your tie is fine."

"But you said we were just going to meet a few friends and family. I don't see what all the rush is about. If we're a half hour or so late what's the big deal? They can eat tasteless cheese on limp crackers without us. I've been to more than my share of these kind of things as faculty get-togethers."

"Yes, well this is a small town and they don't treat lateness as an asset."

"Relax, I'll explain that the tardiness is all my fault. It's not as though anything depended on our being there at a particular time."

"Would you just do this one thing for me?"

"All right, all right. I don't suppose you have any black shoe dye? If not, I can run down to the drug store on the corner and be back in a minute. What's the matter? This isn't anything more that just a casual thing is it?" He dawdles at the mirror.

"David! Please."

"I think I should get a haircut. There's a barber just up the street isn't there?"

"David if we leave right now, I promise, I promise, I promise I'll never ask you for anything ever again.

"I don't for a moment believe that, but I'll settle for some straight answers."

In shock, she trembles with the words, "A…ll right, but not now, David pleeeeeease."

"No pressure. Whenever you're ready, I'll listen."

He follows her out the door, lagging behind like a recalcitrant child.

* * * * * *

In the semi shadows of the barn, Estelle buttons her blouse and smiles down at Bud, still sprawled in the hay, his pants unbuttoned.

"You wouldn't be Italian by any chance?" She looks at her watch. "Oh, we have to get to the church. We're almost too late as it is."

"What do you mean? It's not until eight o'clock tonight."

"They told you that? They must want you there even less than they want me. Come on. Afterward, I can still be your prisoner. You can even tie me up if you like. But if we're going to stop that wedding, we've got to get moving. It's at four and it's already after three."

He takes her hand and pulls her along behind him.

"We can…"

Halfway down the slope he slows abruptly. Estelle slips on wet grass, falls, pulls him down with her. She is unhurt but her skirt is a mess and his slacks are torn on a rock.

"My car. I let my brother take it. There's only his truck."

"Beggars can't be choosers."

They jump into the truck and grind the starter. Angrily it starts with a puff of smoke and backfire.

CHAPTER-21
FAMILY GATHERING

The Porsche pulls to the sidestreet and parks at the curb. Just behind them is a lot filled with cars. Behind the wheel, Michelle turns sideways. "David, I, I hope you won't hate me forever, but…"

He opens his door and steps out. "Not now. Let's go meet these friends and relatives you speak so highly of."

She struggles out of the seat belt. He walks on ahead and she has to hurry to catch up. "Wait, David. I want to talk to you. To try and explain."

"Oh, do hurry. You're the one who didn't want to be late and now you're falling behind."

He purposely increases the length of his stride.

"David you must listen to me!"

"NOW who's bringing the party down? Don't spoil it for me. Whatever this little surprise you have for me, let me enjoy it just as you've planned."

She finally catches up and slipping her hand into his arm, tries to slow him. Instead, he pulls her along with him. She has to run just to maintain station. The tight dress and five inch heels make that a chore. As they turn the corner, she sees her mother and father, the minister and an attractive woman who must be Mrs. Ross. Michelle completely loses her nerve at the sight of the crowd. She breathes deeply, trying not to pass out. Mrs. Ross sees them.

David puts an arm around Michelle's narrow waist and keeps her moving forward. "Mother? Whatever are you doing here?"

Almost in tears, Michelle sobs, "David, I tried to get you to listen, I…"

He doesn't let her finish.

"I thought, mother, you'd have worn your favorite blue dress for such an occasion."

Michelle looks up at him, "David, you…knew?"

"Time enough later for a family reunion. You've gone to a great deal of trouble putting this all together, let us not delay any longer. I trust the minister has been given his instructions? So good to see you again Mr. Morgan, and this must be Mrs. Morgan? It would be my great pleasure to escort you inside. And isn't it traditional for the father of the-bride to see my mother settled?"

Mrs. Morgan sees Michelle wearing for the first time the Paris designed white dress she'd bought for her daughter's someday wedding.

With her mouth open, Michelle watches the others enter the chapel. Paw leads her, robot like, to the front door as David goes to the side entrance. Inside, the black woman from the women's wear store waits as maid of honor. Beside her, the best man, Clem, stands stiffly at attention.

Mr. Morgan and his sons sing an acappella medley of "Dixie" and "The Battle Hymn of the Republic" to a room filled to capacity. The minister smiles, but as the wedding party approaches the altar, all are assaulted by backfiring.

As the truck lurches to a stop in front of the chapel, it continues to pour out oily black smoke.

Bud and Estelle, sweaty and disheveled, burst through the church doors just as the minister gets to the "if anyone has reason why this couple should not be joined" part.

Estelle shouts, "Stop! David, you can't marry this woman."

David frowns, "Estelle? You must be kidding." To Michelle, "Did your father bring his shotgun? I say run them both out on a rail."

To the sheriff, already descending on the intruders, Michelle says, "I think the death penalty is a bit too severe, Uncle Henry. Buuuuut, anything else is proper."

Uncle Henry escorts them both out in cuffs.

CHAPTER-22
WHAT A RECEPTION

At the hotel ballroom, the Morgans play a Bach string quartet, Paw on violin, Maw on bass, Clem on viola, and Luke on cello. The reception is a great success, with the Governor first in the reception line. He hugs and kisses Michelle, his favorite niece. After cake and a waltz together, David and Michelle slip out.

Mrs. Ross smiles and asks Mr. Morgan, "They look so happy together. It is truly a match made in heaven. Tell me, did they meet in church?"

"Something like that." He takes the stage again and calls the boys up. "By way of showing a bit of crossover versatility, this is a number I had the great honor of recording some years ago with Stephane Grappelli and again later with Joe Venutti. It's an improvisation on Prelude in E Minor by Chopin and arranged by Stephane."

They play the number to wild applause and follow it with several light jazz numbers, a few Cole Porter ballads and some Gershwin show tunes. The ballroom entrance is crowded with uninvited hotel guests, drawn to the music.

* * * * * *

Back at the farm, Estelle looks belligerently up into Bud's eyes. "This whole thing is ridiculous. You're as much at fault as am I. Why should I be required to do community service under your supervision?"

"Because I'm a respectable local landowner, while you're a Northern transient."

"But with us here alone together, and you so strong and overpowering... Why, for all I know you could take advantage of me again. Force me to submit to your every sexual desire. Over, and over, and OVER. Why, you might even tie me up."

"Tie you up, how? You could just slip out and…"

"Well, there were lots of ropes up in the stable where probably nobody could hear even if I screamed. And I could show you a couple of knots that are almost impossible to break."

"But you could use the phone in the stable and call for help the first chance you got."

"Oh sure. Like you don't know you could just unplug the line, or take the mouthpiece off. If not, I know how to disconnect the ringer circuit."

CHAPTER-23
A PROFITABLE COTTAGE INDUSTRY

The next day, Maw, dressed like a hillbilly, walks through heavy brush to the weather-beaten tool shed. She unlocks a rusty-looking padlock, opens a rustic door, reaches inside, and turns off a high-tech alarm system. Bright color-corrected lights come on automatically. In the sterile environment, the whir of a commercial air conditioner with humidity control filters the air of all contaminants.

At the spotless white Formica workbench she waits for the elaborate short wave radio to come on and from a modern Scandinavian walnut desk, she takes an order-filled clipboard. The overhead speaker squawks.

"Maw-One callin' Lab One." No answer. She waits patiently.

A few long moments pass, then a voice comes on.

From another shack not far away, "This is Lab 1. Go ahead Maw 1."

She picks up a hand mike. "Clem, I have orders for 10 pieces of A. J., 15 for D. B., 12 for D. C. and 6 for A. H. All grade 1 or above."

"I'm almost out of paper for S.A. and docs. for J. S. but I can use some of that French stuff from 1811."

At Lab 2, a scientific lab of sorts, a white smocked Luke listens at a similar radio set-up. Along one wall, a counter is filled with photographic equipment.

A third wall is filled with original cartoons signed L. Morgan. Another wall is filled with books and boxes marked American paper 1800-1825, American paper 1830-1858, French paper 1805-1812, American Letters & Docs 1735-1855, etc.

On the far wall is a poster showing a man in buckskin, carrying a long-barreled musket, a scowl on his face. In the corner is a poster of Dan'l Boone autograph in two-inch high letters,. Across the bottom, in identical script is "Book 'Em Dan'l." Over the door is a motto in olde English script—CONFERATE RETALIATION.

Maw answers, "No, there's the new material I just brought back. I shipped about a ton or more from Dutch, Belgian and English sources that will work quite well. It should be here in a week or so. It's been wet so it should work well with the Battle of New Orleans stuff."

"Maw, I hope this rush job's not for Virginia. You know those Careys are always slow to pay. They work on our money for ninety days. Everybody else pays within ten days for the extra 1 1/2% discount."

"Yes, but they move as much merchandise as all the others put together."

"Only because they have the Dollywood and Five Flags distribution network."

"That's why they get the big bucks and why we continue to sell to them at wholesale prices instead of going to Ebay."

"Why not keep all that new stuff at LAB 1? I'm running out of room here, and he has the facilities for Dehumidification over there anyway. I'll be home late tonight, I have this lot for D.C. to finish and the rest of that Graceland order."

He turns the set to receive and returns to the light table where he is finishing a bible inscription from Alexander Hamilton.   Above his desk is a poster of Marilyn Monroe.   It too is hand signed with an inscription, all in a feminine script.

> *To Luke, my one and only true love.*
> *If only I were alive today, we would*
> *make such incredible love.   Starting*
> *with you kissing me all over my body.*
> *With my undying love, Marilyn*

CHAPTER-24
NORTHERN LIGHT

A garbage truck goes noisily about its work. The room is completely dark, save for the thin light of dawn sneaking in under the blind at the single bedroom window. It's not time for his alarm to go off, but at the noise, David wakes. He bolts upright, looks out at the familiar view from his Philadelphia apartment. Slowly his pulse returns to normal as he lies back on the bed.

Whew! All a dream. But it seemed so real. I could have sworn...

His hand drops over the side of the bed as his head settles back against the pillow. Into the light from the street, a black and tan coonhound lifts a sleepy head, licks the hand and returns to a watchful slumber.

In the semi-darkness, with her lustrous dark hair spilling onto his cheek, Michelle cuddles closer and mumbles sleepily from the pillow beside him, "You know, darling, I should be quite an asset to you in your work. I did my masters at the Sorbonne on Document Forgery and Literary Counterfeit Detection."

He sighs and tries not to let her see the grin on his face as he whispers, "Actually, you had me at..."

"Ah is a widow."

Vaughn Phelps-Autobiography

With a background in engineering, I attended numerous college writing courses, many seminars and several writer support groups   I scripted screenplays and hundreds of short stories and had published several non-fiction numismatic and horological articles.

Luckily, my TV sit-com episodes weren't accepted, since it takes almost as much time and effort to write a half-hour show as a full-length feature film. Concentrating on feature films was an easy choice. Writing screenplays is fun, but even with encouraging responses from directors and producers, pitching them is not.   So I shifted my attention to short and flash stories.   My first three short story books—SHORT, BUT SWEET, SHORT, NOT SO SWEET and HEADS OR TALES, are available at Amazon.com and the other two will follow shortly.   All contain an average of 20% award winners and others await results.   Along with them, my Ebooks, as released, will be available on Amazon.com.

INTRODUCTION TO E-BOOKS

Please allow me to share with you my Ebooks. Remember; positive word of mouth is the best form of advertisement. All can be purchased on Amazon.com

13-An Hour's Pleasure

16-A Taste of Money

19-A Torch Unseen

21-Black Kat

12-Cold Fire

7-Fantasy Impromptu

3-Fools Rush In

6-Greene's Field

9-Houston, We Have A Problem

2-Independence

17-Just For Kids

4-Just Passin' Thru

1-Liberty

11-Naked We Came

8-Nature Abhors a Vacuum

22-Night Train and Country Gravy

18-One Fist is Iron

20-September 17th

10-Shallow Water

14-The Angel and The Eighteen Wheeler

23-The Big E

15-'37 Indian

5-Writer's Block

ALL my E-books is good.   Some is even
GOODER.

This is an excerpt from my next book.   I hope you enjoy it.

INDEPENDENCE

STORY ADAPTED FROM THE ORIGINAL SCREENPLAY OF THE SAME NAME
By Vaughn Phelps

CHAPTER-1
LIFE ON POTRERO HILL

Manila folder in one hand, martini glass in the other, Tom, a well-dressed man of about fifty, paces. On the wall of this understated, but expensively decorated office/den, are Honorable Discharge U.S. Army, diplomas from U.C. Berkeley, Hastings Law School and various civic awards. The glass drops from his hand as he grabs his chest and crumples to the floor where he lies without moving.

Gladys knocks and enters. "Thomas, darling are you...? Oh my God!" She runs to his side but feels no pulse, dashes to the phone and dials 911.

Minutes later, paramedics place Tom on a stretcher. They carefully ease him through the hallway out to a waiting ambulance. His eyes are open, and he holds an oxygen tank at his side.

Sloping away from this Potrero Hill row house is an unencumbered view of San Francisco Bay.

* * * * * *

The panoramic view of the skyline, starting at the San Francisco Bay Bridge, Ferry Building. Alcatraz, Coit Tower, Marina, Golden Gate Bridge ends at a Sausalito marina filled with expensive houseboats. Aboard one of those, several framed cartoons are autographed to Matt from the best-known cartoonists of the last century. A drawing board and desk filled with sketches and newspaper tear sheets, feature a column, "Squirm & Fidget by Matt Cavanaugh."

Matt, 29, with blond curly hair and muscular build is dressed in polo shirt, gabardine slacks and Italian loafers. Carrying his cell phone, he paces.

"Dad, this is crazy. You've been best friends over thirty-five years. You're going to let a can of paint come between you? Not even that, a spray can nozzle. Let me try and straighten this out. He's been a second father to me." He stops pacing by another wall near a photograph of himself in red tights, white mask and black cape. In the crowd watching from behind cameras, lights and police barriers, a young woman with dark hair and dimples watches Matt's every move. Beside the photo is an original cartoon strip of a mouse in the same pose, dressed the same way. The caption is "Mars Mission Commander" and it's endorsed "to Matt" by Sherry Fielding.

"No, dad." PAUSE "No, dad." PAUSE "I won't argue; there's no point. You're even more stubborn than me." He hangs up.

The photographs on his cluttered desk show two men in olive drab uniform, Cavanaugh, H, L. Capt. and Keppler, T. Capt. with stenciled pocket nametags, standing under a red and white Intelligence Group-4th Army, San Francisco Presidio flag. Another with the same two men, before a 1980 Dodge Charger, smile into the camera, the Golden Gate Bridge in the background. Matt, dials, but gets a busy signal. He paces, tries the phone again, gets the same busy signal. He grabs his coat and heads for the door.

Parking his green MG TD at the bottom of the hill, Matt climbs the steep Potrero district hill, turns in at a wooden step, and without looking, he literally runs into a girl/woman, Erica, sitting on the top step. "Oh, I'm sorry, I didn't see you."

"You're not sorry. You're kind of cute. Now the Dodgers, THEY'RE sorry."

He looks more carefully at the stereotypical Kansas farm girl/girl next-door.

"Your mouth is hanging open. Is that some local fad?"

"No, I..."

"I love the view of the San Francisco Bay on a bright day like this don't you?"

"Yes. Who are you?"

"Why? Don't I look like I belong?"

By his facial expression alone it's clear that he is completely enraptured by her.

"No. I mean yes. Make that a firm yes. Capital yes, affirmative, positive, 10-4."

"I guess when your spring winds down, you'll make sense?"

"Yes. I mean I usually do. Make sense that is. Now, in a completely rational voice and manner may I be so bold as to inquire who you are?"

"Now, in an equally calm and rational tone, I'm Erica Keppler, Tom's daughter."

"Daughter? That can't be."

"Oh? You mean I'm his son and never realized it?"

"No, I mean, it's just that I've known the Kepplers since before I was born. Your dad and mine have been friends most of their lives. They went through junior and high school, college and the army together."

"Your father being?"

"Lawrence Cavanaugh."

"Then do I call you Baby Boy Cavanaugh?"

"No, I'm Matthew, Matt to my friends. And I *know* we're going to be friends."

"Ummmmm...I think I like Baby Boy Cavanaugh better."

"I won't even mind that if you'll explain how it is that we've never met."

"Have you ever been to Independence, Missouri?"

"No."

"Well, there you go. That's why we've never met."

"Oh."

"Your mouth is hanging open again."

"Sorry, it's just that…"

"I guess you hadn't heard. My dad suffered a mild heart attack last Monday."

"No. Is he all right?"

"Yes. He's here at home. The doctor says there should be no long-term effect. Not if he behaves himself."

"I'll go in and—"

114

"He's resting right now. Tomorrow would be better."

"How is it in all the years I've known your father, he never mentioned a daughter?"

"He and mother divorced when I was only three. It was a bitter separation. She won't even allow any photographs of him around. I imagine Gladys also feels more comfortable without daily reminders of mom or me around."

"But you've maintained contact with your dad?"

"We've written or spoken at least once a month for over twenty years."

"What do you do there in Missouri?"

With a big smile, "I'm a hit woman for the mob."

"Come-on, be serious."

"Okay, that usually drives off the faint of heart. If you won't buy that, I'm a travel agent from Independence, Missouri."

"Can we go someplace and talk, get a cup of coffee, maybe get married?"

She laughs. She does it easily, naturally. "We can talk right here."

"It gets windy here on the hill."

"There's coffee inside."

"That's a problem. Your dad bought a defective three-dollar spray can of paint from my dad's hardware store. They had words, and now they're suing each other. I was going to try and back it up to reality, but right now is maybe not the best time."

Okay, I guess we could go for coffee. I get cabin fever inside anyway. But I've always enjoyed visiting San Francisco."

"What about the other?"

She stands up, laughs again. "No, let's not get married today."

"I'm free all day tomorrow."

They take a table at a Pier 39 patio café that offers a vista of the Golden Gate. With Alcatraz in the background, they watch big ships and small sailboats, drink coffee and eat chocolate filled desserts.

"My name is Matthew David Cavanaugh, I'm a columnist for the Chronicle, I own my own houseboat and car. I save most of my salary. I have all my own hair and teeth, my table manners are tolerable, I'm kind to old ladies and small dogs. I eat all my vegetables, drink only in moderation, and aspirin is the only drug of choice."

"You're not making a computer dating video."

"I'm trying."

At the Hyde Street Pier, Matt holds her hand and they stroll through the Cannery, the Maritime Museum and climb to the top of Coit Tower. Erica looks at her watch. He doesn't give her a chance to say, "It's late."

"It's dinnertime. Do you like Chinese, Mexican, Hungarian, French, or Scandinavian food?"

"Well..."

You could just leave it up to me. I know the city backward and forward. How about seafood?"

"I love seafood, but I'm not dressed for any place fancy."

"You look just great to me. Better than great, great times five."

"I could change, meet you someplace later."

"Why not change now? I'll drive you home and wait."

"I'm staying at the Holiday Inn and I still have to pack."

"I could take you there and… wait, what do you mean pack?"

"I've been here for almost a week. I have to get back to work."

"Wrong! I'm not losing you now. It's not fair, you being here that long and we've just met."

"I'm a big girl. I can manage. And it's not my fault that you let me languish here alone and unwanted."

"You could pass for sixteen, but that's not the point. *I* want you and will never again allow you to languish or be alone, nor feel unwanted."

"I'm on an early morning flight. I'd have to be back by ten."

"No problem. What time's your flight?"

"One A.M., but I have to check out of the hotel and say good-bye to dad."

"If you check out now, we can have dinner, then see your dad on the way to the airport."

"Take me to the hotel. I'll change, then we'll see."

CHAPTER-2
TIME FOR COMMITTMENT

Matt and Erica have dinner at Sausalito's dockside. Even to diners at adjacent tables, it's evident that Matt is proposing again in earnest.

"I just don't do things like that. But I've had fun. Maybe if we had more time..."

"We'll take more time. I have a lot of connections. I could get you a job at a dozen Travel Agency's right here."

"Can't. But if you're ever in Buffalo..."

"I thought you said you were from Independence."

"I meant that's where I grew up. My mother still lives there."

"Why do you have to run off just when we're getting to know each other?"

"I'm not running off."

With seeming panic, he grabs her left hand. "You're not married?"

"No."

"Have a serious boyfriend?"

Laughing, "No, but I'm a working girl and I have to meet a tour group in Banff."

He thinks less than the time of a good blink and says, "I've always wanted to see Banff..fff. I'll go with you. I can write my column from there. Given time and opportunity I'll wear you down."

"There's no time for you to pack and make reservations."

"I always carry an extra shirt in the car and I'll buy anything else I need. You're a travel agent. Can't you handle the reservation and flight details for me?"

"Yes, but..."

"What I may lack in charm, I make up for in persistence."

"You're...not lacking in charm. It's just that..."

"Look, my dad's the only person I ever met who's more stubborn than me. So if you don't want the commission, I'll buy my ticket at the airport, and if the hotel is full, I'll sleep on your balcony."

Erica shrugs her shoulders, phones and makes notes. Even from a distance, it's obvious that she's arranging a ticket for him on her flight.

Much later that night, Erica, in a summery dress, enters her father's house while Matt arranges and rearranges her one suitcase in his diminutive trunk. While she's gone, he dials his cell phone. "Dad, I'm in love and I'm getting married." PAUSE. "No, she's not a stew. She's...I'll explain later." PAUSE "I know, it came as a shock to me too. Can you pick up my car at Airport Valet Parking? And cancel my golf date with Doug?"

CHAPTER-3
PARIS IS GOOD ANYTIME

At an outdoor cafe, well-dressed, distinguished looking men drink demitasse coffee, speak in French and gesticulate over everything. They stop talking as casual strollers pass. One of the men with wavy silver grey hair wears a boutonniere and waves his hands less than the others. The Eiffel Tower dominates the background; spring blossom-filled street vendor's carts the foreground.

* * * * * *

At The San Francisco International Airport, a well-built man, completely bald, wearing yellow shooting glasses, scans a Forbes magazine at a notions kiosk. He marks certain lines with a highlighter pen, leaves it and an envelope with the clerk. The clerk opens the envelope; it's filled with twenties and a note.

At the same kiosk a half-hour later, Erica buys sour dough French bread, salted sunflower seeds and a Forbes magazine. She pays with three two-dollar bills. The clerk switches her Forbes for the marked copy. Bald Man watches as Erica and Matt enter the "Wheels Up" cocktail lounge together. When they leave and head for their gate. Bald Man enters the lounge and leans close to the bartender. "That good looking fella with the foxy young blonde. I've seen them someplace. Are they local?"

The bartender keeps rearranging the bottles on the top shelf. Bald Man folds a twenty in half lengthwise and holds it out. "Bud."

The bartender hands him a frosty glass, takes the twenty and waits.

"Keep the change."

"I've never seen the girl before, but he's in here with his buddy all the time." He puts a chilled Bud on the bar. "They always have new chicks in tow."

Bald Man produces another twenty. He doesn't get another beer, only an answer.

"His buddy's a golf hustler and I think he's a cop. I've spotted a badge when he pays, but I never gave it much attention."

With a questioning expression, a man holds up a paper left on the bar. The bartender waves it off. "Take it. I never read newspapers. They're too full of misery."

Bald Man slides another twenty across the bar. "Do you know his name?"

"His buddy's Doug something. His is either Nat or Mat, something like that. That's all I know, fella. When it's busy in here, I can't..."

Bald Man finishes his beer and slides off the stool. "Okay, thanks. I guess I was mistaken. I got no cops as friends."

"You an' me both, buddy."

Bald Man leaves, but writes the details in a spiral notebook.

* * * * * *

At Sea/Tac, Matt and Erica wait beside the Can-Am dock. On the departure board, Flight #617 for Calgary/Banff is expected to be an hour late. While they wait, passengers are offered a free breakfast of toast and coffee.

"Damn." Erica frowns, "No, thank you. We're already two hours behind schedule."

"We're very sorry, miss." She doesn't look or sound it. The woman leaves and Matt grins. "Isn't this great? You can see how well we deal with adversity, working together as a team."

Erica turns drooping eyelids in his direction, but can't manage a smile.

* * * * * *

At the same time, Boutonniere walks along the Quebec riverbank. There are barges, commercial boats, but no pleasure craft in sight. He climbs into a black Caddy that pulls alongside. The Caddy weaves through traffic of predominantly American cars driven by polite Canadian drivers. The Caddy stops at St Benedict and a black robed man is escorted to the back seat.

"Monsignor, I am delighted you were available. I know how busy you must be right now."

The Cleric nods, climbs in and the Caddy again turns into heavy traffic. Banners in French and English—

"Bastille Day Celebration"

fly.

* * * * * *

John Falstaff, San Francisco Chronicle Editor, Games and Columns desk, answers the phone, and listens.

"Tom's daughter? Tom doesn't have... You can't be..."

He hangs up and goes to a calendar board. There are ANAGRAMS marked—use-Cavanaugh.

He writes "Wedding bells for Matt Cavanaugh," then dials a novelty shop. He makes notes and smiles.

* * * * * *

Just after dawn, Matt leaves his Banff room, walks the fifteen feet up the corridor and knocks at Erica's door. She covers her head with a pillow, tries to shut out the light, the noise and the day. He finds a maid. "My fiancée has a tendency to take sleeping pills. I've tried to get her to stop, but she doesn't listen. Can we check on her, please?"

The Maid lets him in, but stays with him. He goes to Erica's side. "Come on, darling, you'll sleep the whole day away if you're not careful."

"That was the plan."

"You don't mean that."

The maid adds, "You should listen to your man, eh? He only has your best interest at heart."

"What?"

"I said he only wants the best for you, don'tcha know?"

She leaves the lovebirds alone.

"What did that maid...?"

"A remarkable judge of character, but enough about her. Think about us. It's a glorious day. The sun is out, the sky is blue and I've hired a horse and carriage to show you the country."

Erica pulls the covers over her head.

"I'm a travel agent. I've seen the country."

He pulls the covers down.

"But not with me."

While she showers and dresses, Matt thumbs through her Forbes and sees the highlighted portions, plus letters and numbers in the margins in her hand. By the time she's ready, the sky is leaden and it's started snowing. She looks out the window and frowns.

He grins like a schoolboy let out of school for the day. "This is better. I've changed the carriage for a sled. It's even more romantic."

At the hotel's stables, Matt bundles Erica into a blanket so tightly she can hardly move. The passing scenery is from a Currier and Ives print.

Matt and Erica stroll through the Banff lobby. He holds her hand. "I'm really not crazy. I'm a conservative guy and I've never done anything like this before. My only defense is that if we only meet the right person once, then a normal courtship is impossible. With you two thousand miles away, my only chance is to press my advantage. Besides, I get triple odds that way."

"I don't say YOU are crazy, but THIS is crazy. What did you write about me?"

"Ah, you can read my column tomorrow."

"But I want to know now. You didn't mention my name or…?"

"Name, occupation, itinerary and my complete devotion to you. Soon you'll be receiving letters from my millions of loyal readers pleading my case and urging you to accept the heart of this, your love slave. Okay, I exaggerated a bit, my six fans."

"How could they write to me? You don't even know my address."

"I'll have all the details by the time we reach Hamilton."

"I was wrong.   You ARE crazy."

"Love is a fine form of madness."

That's it.   If I gave you any more, you wouldn't have to buy the book.   *Vaughn*